羅得彰 著譯
Poems and Translation by Te-chang Mike Lo

台灣日・南非夜

Taiwan Days,
South Africa Nights

羅得彰漢英雙語詩集
Mandarin-English

台灣詩叢 • Taiwan Poetry Series 20

【總序】詩推台灣意象

叢書策畫／李魁賢

　　進入21世紀，台灣詩人更積極走向國際，個人竭盡所能，在詩人朋友熱烈參與支持下，策畫出席過印度、蒙古、古巴、智利、緬甸、孟加拉、尼加拉瓜、馬其頓、秘魯、突尼西亞、越南、希臘、羅馬尼亞、墨西哥等國舉辦的國際詩歌節，並編輯《台灣心聲》等多種詩選在各國發行，使台灣詩人心聲透過作品傳佈國際間。

　　多年來進行國際詩交流活動最困擾的問題，莫如臨時編輯帶往國外交流的選集，大都應急處理，不但時間緊迫，且選用作品難免會有不週。因此，興起策畫【台灣詩叢】雙語詩系的念頭。若台灣詩人平常就有雙語詩集出版，隨時可以應用，詩作交流與詩人交誼雙管齊下，更具實際成效，對台灣詩的國際交流活動，當更加順利。

　　以【台灣】為名，著眼點當然有鑑於台灣文學在國際間名目不彰，台灣詩人能夠有機會在國際努力開拓空間，非為個人建立知名度，而是為推展台灣意象的整體事功，期待開創台灣文學的長久景象，才能奠定寶貴的歷史意義，台灣文學終必在世界文壇上佔有地位。

　　實際經驗也明顯印證，台灣詩人參與國際詩交流活動，很受
重視，帶出去的詩選集也深受歡迎，從近年外國詩人和出版社與
本人合作編譯台灣詩選，甚至主動翻譯本人詩集在各國文學雜誌或
詩刊發表，進而出版外譯詩集的情況，大為增多，即可充分證明。

　　承蒙秀威資訊科技公司一本支援詩集出版初衷，慨然接受
【台灣詩叢】列入編輯計畫，對台灣詩的國際交流，提供推進力
量，希望能有更多各種不同外語的雙語詩集出版，形成進軍國際
的集結基地。

目次

在淡水的詩人

倉庫還記得
渴望開門並吞噬
來自遙遠的喜悅
回報詩人們
三百多天
一直在培養的情緒

淡水河匆忙地趕進來
問候虎崗的老朋友們
潮水因來自遠方
文字愛好者之讚賞漲升
帶來新的讚美詞在
讓她臉色羞紅

陸地和海洋的情感比比皆是
再隨著退潮離開
去傳播淡水之美
像候鳥，詩將在明秋歸來
提醒人們在日常生活中
被遺忘的美麗

2019.09

淡水

觀音山接送
被金屬蛇吐出的訪客
有金屬鞘套之寺廟
守護遊客和當地人
歡迎來到淡水

河浪跟路人輕輕揮手
有些人被歷史吸引
其他是被純淨之美麗
全體都著迷
淡水河說，在此跟您問候

紅堡，淡水歷史之
年長貴婦在旁觀看，寬容地
接受於她上面、內部及周遭好玩的遊客
讓她用幾世紀的故事來向你介紹
無法磨滅的淡水回憶錄

孩子們圍著訪客
渴望學習和吸取他們的熱情
他們的小小世界很小
但是大到可以容納所有的人
看看淡水的未來

詩歌在空中飄揚
在人群中游泳
異國情調和當地感覺之貢奉
鞏固詩歌之鄉
讓他們的文字在淡水引導你

2019.09

海灘上的情書

甲殼類動物拼的異形字圖信在招手
試圖理解情書中的字體
寫給大海、給天空、給自己也在寫信的鄰居
來自大海但被潮池困住的情緒
養育著太晚起床而回不了家的魚

我看到拖在我身後的腳印
與螃蟹晚餐的剩菜錯雜
沙灘上一個蒼白的八足跑手在衝刺
漂浮在海風中，為了在潮汐奪走
它的信之前趕回家把信寫完

遙遠的海洋地平線上之夕陽
與蒼白的月亮幽影在爭奪天空中的空檔
阿波羅讀了信就笑著退幕
阿提米絲匆忙趕上來要在
波塞頓把信從她的視野刪掉前看完

2019.09

櫻花（一）

粗糙、老人手指似的樹枝
在指節上靈巧地產出粉紅花朵
像街頭魔術師一樣，賣藝吸引注意力
他們產生的收入不是銅幣和紙鈔
而是拍照手機的數量
在線上分享，儘管鮮花永遠不會
看到無數的讚

一條人河蜿蜒流過樹木
沒有提供養分
只有空虛雜音的激流
一隻孤獨的蒼白蝴蝶奔飛經過我的鼻子
不耐煩地飄飛
沒人關心它驅趕人群的努力
也許它需要將嗡嗡的蜜蜂近鄰叫醒
去趕走逢迎者
將不自然的花園恢復至原始狀態

2020.04

櫻花（二）

拿出舉起手機
點擊拍下無數的照片
框置粉紅和豔紅的花朵
於最理想的位置
把花像明星一樣對待
植物狗仔隊一年一次
會帶著鏡頭和煩厭的喋喋不休
來騷擾當日的寵兒

所有人關注盛開的花朵
只關心眼前當下
但是生活很少是亮麗的
真正的明星朦朧地閃耀
褪色枯萎的花朵
擺脫流行的束縛
由發芽的綠苞加冕

每年甦醒的奇蹟
不受崇拜和傾慕

2020.05

賞鯨·賞海

小船腰肢搖擺
一位咖啡師攪動
在無限大杯的海軍藍咖啡
打出泡沫
品嚐白色船殼沖泡的衝鼻鹽水
飛魚婆娑起舞作調味
蹦飛來問我是否是常客

閃電閃爍，雷聲咆哮
昏昏欲睡的遠山呼出一縷雲霧
灑下溫柔的眼淚
餵給口渴的土地

解了乾喉之渴
我仍渴望有心靈的萬能藥
以消除城市的人工調味劑
我在找我來拜訪的鯨魚

但是只有海豚來玩
我不好意思拒絕他們的善意
所以用相機的喀嚓聲回應
他們嘀嗒的歌聲

2020.07

揭

揭开
我们膚淺、染色的視覺
黑檀木或白象牙色
健康的粉紅或太陽輕吻的黃色
色譜被忽略
對於歡騰的病毒
我們都不過是個遊樂場

揭下口罩
我鬆了一口氣
每次溫熱並令人窒息的呼吸
讓真理的鏡頭起霧
我擦掉人造的露水
想著是否也必須為其他人這樣做
以讓他們看透誤傳資訊

已被揭露的
橙色謊言和覆著焦糖糖衣的數字
加甜並加工讓大眾可吞嚥
但是人造甜味劑已不能稀釋
那些不再繼續被短視常態
催眠的人之闇黑怒火

2020.09

口罩

藍色的、綠色的、黑色的、粉紅
一系列的保護色彩
無法掩飾憂慮的表情
為自己、家族、國家
WHO 敢在被撕裂的保護傘下
施加偏見和歪斜的政治

直髮、短髮、捲髮、染色的
髮型與口罩不搭配
讓人想到病毒成為國王之前的時光
WHO 以侮辱真理者為登基之作
並在國王之致死訊息
把他帶走前逼迫悔改

擔心的表情、驚慌的動作、不合理的汙名、擔憂
原始的負面情緒遠遠超過關心
無法被口罩隱藏並扼制

WHO 誤傳資訊並誤導世界
錯賀那些最不應該得到讚美的人
一切為了最低俗的權宜之計

黑暗蔓延

黑暗的蔓延不再是在夜深人靜時
在耀眼的陽光下一目了然
不怕人
由只會尋求關注的浮華小丑
和扮演上帝的絨毛玩物帶頭
協助和慈恩
生命的竊賊在公開場合疾走
不受牆壁和屋頂的阻礙
竊取我們的幸福感
將街道變成凡人不敢踏足之
空曠的道路和人行道
他無視法律界限和屏障
興高采烈地跳上輪船和飛機
傳播沒人要的有害惡意福音
獲得不情願的追隨者哀嘆他的到來
自由的竊賊是最自由的
當他在我們之間移動時沒有受到挑戰

在行動和參與中掌握我們的自由
在病毒統治的土地上引入沮喪的嚎叫
病毒肆意跳舞
他不關心政治宣傳和假消息
（一個具有致命幽默感的開笑話者）
坐著這些媒介
無定形的腳踐踏著當權者
讓所有人提防竊盜和那些
在搶劫狂潮中有選擇性失明和失聰之人

銜尾蛇

我們用減毒性病毒來預防病毒
我們為拯救自然而產生更多的垃圾
這極度諷刺壓在我的靈魂上
但沒有靈魂的小丑和鐵腕的權力販子
使用量化寬鬆來減輕罪惡感
我們毫無羞恥地欺騙自己

騙子詐騙自己人
從無意義的數字中找到滿足感
當你的財產超過一生的總秒數
生活變成了一場毀滅他人的遊戲

大自然的使者使勁
將工業複合體
煞住
掠奪和黑金之依賴
暫停了一下

生命就回游到運河之城
悠哉在空街上散步
這個星球的主人正忙著吞噬自己

2021.03

過年

躲開老街的喧鬧
遠離輕軌的人潮
靜靜的淡水
比鄉下還鄉下

雙車道的馬路
整年假裝苗條
車子都回家過年時
它才承認
「其實我是四線道」

躺在柏油路上的流浪狗
傻哈哈地瞪著我騎腳踏車
新年舊年都無所謂
這邊的海風跟細雨
只有我跟它共享

鞭炮怒放
櫻花怒放
傳統與大自然競賽
看誰的新年活動
較吸引人

2021.03

我知道

我知道
從眉毛的弧形
微笑的雙眼
角邊的小皺紋
那是你

我知道
從含糊的口音
從我記不得你臉的
下半部看來是怎樣
你在乎

我知道
此時不是我們期望的
不是我們希望的
但我們期待讓我們
渡過此時就是希望

我知道
科學與理智
不是政治和民粹主義
將是戰勝
看不見的敵人之武器

這一切我都知道
因此我知道我們會
熬過生命的輪迴
而再重新開始

2021.07-08

陰天

銀色的雨劃過灰色的天空
是回憶的眼淚
來自記得過去的造訪之城市
我試著撿起閃閃發光的天國寶石
但它們從我的手指間溜走了。
哦！它們不屬於我
我讓它們留在那兒
希望別人
可以撿起來
去享受我曾知的
那種快樂

2020.03（-23.04）

淡秋・水

淡秋
的細雨追著
颱風而來
驅逐酷溫
卻趕不走
口罩下的熱氣

淡江
的學生
隨著秋日
回游校園
虛擬的教室
無法代替
實體的熱情

淡水
的老街

靠在河水
的肩膀上
小攤私語
感嘆只有病毒
在街上迴盪

2021.09

南非落陽

血紅太陽落回
乾涸的地平線
將我的痛苦抽吸並滴點
至那片應該從
不人道的人類
獲得更多憐憫的土地上
財物和財富拿去吧
但是你不能將他的生命
賣給任何生命販子
所以你是為了什麼
把沒有傷害你的靈魂
從身體中剝離出來

2021.09-11

兩地

人造的時間
鞭驅著生活
我活在平行的時間線上
隨著淡水醒來
看著前一晚的
非洲凌晨
彎月
疑惑地看著
站在冷風中的我
做夢的奢侈
泡沫化
杉葉嗦嗦
與夜鴞交流
此刻的夜色催眠
刻塑至心中眼中
活在黑暗大陸的靈魂
支持遠東的軀體

殘酷的現實
割裂兩地
的安全感

2021.09

秋老虎

今年的秋老虎
是短命的
它是否找了
柴郡貓拜師
只留下嘲諷的笑容
或者它被
人為氣候變化獵殺
皮毛不留

2021.09

南非拜佛

在異國他鄉迷路的神祇
蓮花坐，慧眼望入
南非高地草原
祂找不到自己
因為甚至連祂都不會發
此地的音──Bronkhorstspruit
我因傳統並尊重那些把祂帶到這裡
的人而鞠躬磕頭
信仰現在是一個空虛的概念
但我不是為了我的心靈
而是為我離開的太早
雙親做請求
以免他們迷失在長住
卻陌生的土地上

2021.09-11

黑森林蛋糕

我對困擾
我睡夢的黑森林蛋糕
一直渴望
提醒我我錯過的東西
叉子切透
鮮奶油和黑巧克力
反射性淚水和唾液
弄濕了我的臉
因為品嚐熟悉的舊味道之
分泌物是喜或悲
我不知道也不管
只知道天堂滾落在我的舌頭上

2021.09-11

草地（一）

台灣的草地帶著敵意
身邊陪著野草影武者
以防意料之外的赤腳
忽然暗殺翠綠之君
因為他們跟人類友善的親戚
已被滅絕

2021.09-11

草地（二）

南非的草地乾枯而立
在遠方的視野中已跟棕土而混
我的赤腳踩上他們今年的屍體
懷念著他們明春的新生
也許我的樂觀和希望
會和它們一起重新發芽

2021.09-11

飛翔

地瓜形狀的民主
羽毛尚未豐滿但正在努力飛行
承載著那些在它上面和遠離它的人
之希望、夢想和期待
向代達洛斯學習
建造自己的翅膀並飛翔
但不要忽視自由
不要把自由的溫暖
跟那些沒有翅膀的人
之激熱情緒混淆

2022.02

小確幸

在冬天的寒冷中醒來
在無情的陽光下汗流浹背
我很感恩
因為在這島上
我是活著的

便利商店從每個角落往外瞪
打瞌睡的通勤者乘坐向外延伸的幹線
我很感激
因為在這島上
我可以自由移動

未經審查的資訊用
無線網路的翅膀向我飛來
我很開心
因為在這島上
我可以知道真實的世界

自由行走、交談和思考
這些不是小確幸
當它們在這島上
滋潤靈魂

2022.02

夢・愛

我是完整
我是失去
我走在熟悉的路上
以未知告終
你曾在那裡
帶著我不知道
我遺失的碎片
我試著撿起來
但它們不屬於我
愛留在夢裡
我的外表完整無瑕
我的內在支離破碎

2022.02

原名

淡水的淡水
輕輕地路過
在觀音山腳下
的紅樹林盤桓
黏泥上閒逛的
提琴手蟹
揮著樂器問我
詩人來了沒

桂花巷的桂花
又錯過了來訪的詩情
但鄉民的熱情
在他們的臉上
如花苞綻放
迷人的鄉情詩意
在詩路上飄散

水源里的水源
躲在大屯山的雲霧中
我找不到它
只能問田裡的皎白筍
清澈的流水
是否甘之如飴

2022.09

傳詩

無上限的知識
在黃舊書頁上
在嶄新雲端上
看著新成員加入它們
生氣勃勃的詩泉
帶著上百年經驗
走入虎崗上的殿堂
詩意不再是一時一刻
而是無限的一部分

2022.09

燈塔

登上已不存在的燈塔
眺望過去
疲憊鏽骨的炮台
堅持守護
鄉莊的文藝
在真情的歌聲中
看到
流露
對未來的懷念
在極權的濃霧中
成為文化的燈塔
照亮詩情海陸

2022.09

華爾茲政治

一二三
左一步
右一步
退回一步
政府跳著
華麗的腳步
總是在移動
永遠沒進步

一二三
承諾物價肯定不會上漲
提高生活成本
時代不一樣當作藉口
不要失去節奏

一二三
墮胎不是一種選擇

槍支等於自由
正義被政治化
繼續跳著華爾茲

一二三
左、右、後
我們又轉又繞
這支舞什麼時候結束？

2022.10 (-2023.04)

藍與金

藍天
黃金田
被灰煙薰染
溪流般的坦克
士兵
還有飛彈
和從來不是報喜的消息
產出他們自己和那些
被認為是他們的兄弟姐妹和表堂兄弟姐妹之死亡

不正義和喪失之小河
直播到線上洪流
用鮮血和政治宣傳
澆灌歐洲的麵包籃
現在是一個破碎的篩子試圖保留
和平的碎片
麥浪淒涼地對

喁喁細語的藍色溪流
和金色的寧靜日子搖手告別
但它知道曾經贏得的獨立
再也不會被
騎馬獨裁者的足蹄踐踏

2022.12

節日──冬季（一）

東北風帶來了
在沒有生命的霧霾中
被不死病毒汙染的信件
還有他知道誰是淘氣或乖巧
的消息
但聖人對豪豬之島有警惕
並引導他的馴鹿繞過導彈
凝視著生不出安心的
耶穌誕生劇

無限循環的頌歌聲
「第一個聖誕」由毫無情緒的機器演唱
商業化的異教節日
繼續吸引更多異教徒
不點蠟燭
而是滑螢幕尋找節日氣氛

聖誕節不是那麼快樂的時候當
世上平安，眾人彼此友好相待
只能在編造的故事之
頁面上找到。

2023.01

節日──冬季（二）

潮濕和風猛吹著人群

不懈地向著自由衝鋒

忘記死亡的自由

不戴口罩而尖喊的自由

掙脫微生物壓迫者

束縛他們的鐐銬

用空白的紙張慶祝

用從摩天大樓和橋梁噴湧而出的

煙花為記憶消毒

逆著蜂擁而至的身軀反游

在心神中的煙火

悄悄對自己喊新年快樂

2023.01

台灣日・南非夜

我醒來與
跟我同樣膚色的族群移動
我的思緒順著並逆向與人群游動
11000 公里外的南非高原雷雨
比剛才飆過去差點壓到
我的腳趾之摩托車
在我耳邊響起更大的聲音

福爾摩莎的陽光和濕氣
耗盡我的意志
我想要藍花楹樹下
讓我涼下來、恢復活力
的非洲陰影
像安珀之梅林
行走地球與影子世界
我在兩個世界中移動
躲避未知的自己之死亡

試圖遠離仇恨和歷史
新體液和敘事的創始
代替疲憊的思緒和血脈
從內部創造之新的人
乃為舊的我之克隆人
穿著相同的皮膚
對自己用舊的真實
和虛構回憶洗腦
我關掉我的燈
打開冷氣
夢著困擾著我過去的生活
的滾動停電

我生活在清醒和睡眠
的二元性中
台灣日南非夜
南非日台灣夜

夜日
南台灣非
二元性在我身上統一

2022.12 (-2023.04)

作者／譯者簡介

　　羅得彰，1978 年出生於台灣。小時候隨家人移民到南非居住 25 多年，並獲得了分子醫學博士。回台尋找他的台灣性後，經過一連串的機緣巧合，讓他的職涯轉向口筆譯／教學和寫作。他目前居住在台灣北部的淡水，致力於進一步提高自己的寫作技巧。

【英語篇】
Taiwan Days,
South Africa Nights

Foreword: using poetry to promote the imagery of Taiwan

Lee Kuei-Shien, curator of The Taiwan Poetry Series

After the turn of the millennium, Taiwanese poets have become more proactive in stepping onto the international stage. With enthusiastic support and participation of poet friends, I had planned and made every effort to attend international festivals held in India, Mongolia, Cuba, Chile, Myanmar, Bangladesh, Nicaragua, Macedonia, Peru, Tunisia, Vietnam, Greece, Romania, and Mexico. I had also compiled various poetry collections like "Voices from Taiwan" to be published in various countries, so that the heartfelt voices of the Taiwanese poets can indeed be heard through their works and spread internationally.

Perhaps the most annoying issue when carrying out poetry exchanges internationally in the past years, was the fact that having to quickly edit and prepare poetry collections to be taken along to these festivals. Most of the time this was done at a moment's notice, where there was an obvious time pressure, and handling of the works may not be to the author's satisfaction. Thus, the thought of planning a bilingual poetry series like this "Taiwan Poetry Series" arose. If Taiwanese poets normally make a plan to publish bilingual poetry collections, then these can be used at any time where poetry exchange and poets' networking can proceed simultaneously. This will produce more effective results, and allows for a smoother process when using Taiwanese poems to carry out international exchanges.

The inclusion of 'Taiwan' in the series is the obvious draw point, and is necessary due to the lack of presence Taiwan has in international literature. Taiwanese poets having opportunities to make headway internationally should not be doing it for the sake of establishing their own fame, but as part of the overall effort to promote the imagery of Taiwan, all in the hope of establishing the long-term standing of Taiwanese literature on the global stage. Only then, can there is long-lasting meaning, and Taiwanese literature's position of importance in world literature can be assured.

Past experience has also shown that Taiwanese poets received much attention when they participated in international poetry events and exchanges, and the poetry collections they brought with them were very much welcomed. Further empirical proof comes from the fact that I have worked with numerous foreign poets and publishers to collate and translate Taiwanese poetry collection with greater frequency; there have even been increasing number of occasions where, without my prompting, some of my works were translated and published in various foreign literature or poetry magazines, which eventually led to the publication of entire collections in other languages.

I would like to express my appreciation to Showwe Information Co. Ltd., whose initial endeavor of supporting the publication of poetry collections turned into a willingness to take on the "Taiwan Poetry Series" in their long-term publishing strategy. This provide a much needed impetus for exchange using Taiwanese poetry across the globe, and hopefully there will be more bilingual poetry collection featuring languages outside of English in the future, which will create a solid foundation for Taiwanese poetry to propel itself onto the international stage.

Translated by Te-chang Mike Lo

CONTENTS

Poets in Tamsui

The warehouse remembers
Eager to open up and swallow up
The joyful feelings coming from far
Returning the emotions
That has been nurtured in poets
For three hundred-odd days

Tamsui River hurries in
Greeting long-time friends of the Tiger Hills
The tide swelling with admiration
From lovers of words near and far
Brining new words of praises to paint
Her in a rosy blush.

Feelings abound in land and the sea
And leaving again with the ebb
To spread the beauty of Tamsui

Migratory birds, the poems shall return

In the next fall as reminders of beauty

Forgotten in daily lives

Tamsui

Guanyin Mountain chauffeurs in
Visitors disgorged by the metal snake
The metal-sheathed temple
Stands guard over tourist and locals alike
Welcome to Tamsui

The river waves gently at passersby
Some are intrigued by the history
Other by the pure beauty
Enchanted visitors all
Greeting, says the River of Tamsui

The Red Fort, the old dame of
Tamsui history watches, tolerant
Of playful visitors on, in and around
Let her regale you with tales of the centuries
The unerasable memoirs of Tamsui

Children encircles the visitors
Eager to learn and absorb their passion
Their little world is small
Yet big enough to embrace all
See the future of Tamsui

Poems aflutter in the air
Swimming through the crowds
Offerings of foreign love and local feeling
To ensconce the home of poetry
Let their words guide you in Tamsui

Love Letters on the Beach

The xenographic letters spelt out by the crustacean beckons

Trying to understand the fonts within the love letters

To the sea, to the sky, to their neighbours who write their own

The feelings of the sea trapped in the tidal pools

Nurturing the fishes who woke up too late to go home

I see the dragged out footprints behind me

Mixing with the sandy leftovers of the crab's dinner

A pale eight-legged racer sprint on the sand

Floated by the sea breeze, rushing to get home

To finish his letter before the tide take it

The setting sun in the distant marine horizon

The pale ghost of the moon vying for the opening in the sky

Apollo has read the letters and retires with a smile

Artemis rushes forth to catch the words

Before Poseidon removes them from her view

Cherry Blossoms I

The gnarled, old-man fingered branches

Dexterously producing pink blossoms on their knuckles

Like a street magician busking for attention

The income they generate are not coins and notes

But the number of cellphone snapping pictures

Sharing online, although the flowers will never

See the myriads of thumb ups

A river of people winds and flow past the trees

Offering no nutrients

But a torrent of inane murmurs

A lone pale butterfly dart past my nose,

Fluttering in annoyance

For no one cares about its effort to shoo people away

Mayhaps it need to rouse its buzzing apian neighbours

To chase the hangers-on away

And return the unnatural garden to its pristine state

Cherry Blossoms II

Cellphones out and held up

Clicking and snapping countless pictures

Framing the pink and red blossoms

In the perfect position

Treating the flowers like stars

The botanical paparazzi come

But once a year to harass the darlings of the day

With camera lenses and harassing chatters

All are focused on the flowers in bloom

Only caring about the here and now

But life is rarely pretty

The true star shines dimly

The fading and wilted flowers, unfettered by popularity

Crowned by the budding greens

The annual miracle that come to life

Is not worshipped and adored

Whale Watching ·
Ocean Appreciation

The boat sways

A barista stirring

The infinite cup of navy blue coffee

To froth

Taste the tangy brine spilled by the white hull

Tempered with the dance of the flying fish

Glide hopping to ask if I was a frequent visitor

Lightning flashes, thunder roars

The sleepy mountain exhales a plume of clouds

Shedding a gentle shower of tears

To feed the parched earth

Dry throat slaked

I still yearn for the mental panacea that removes

The artificial flavourants of the city from which I came

I look for the whales I came to visit

But only dolphins came to play

Embarrassed to decline their goodwill

I clicked my camera to respond to

Their clucking song

Unmask

Unmask

The facile colour-tinted vision we possess

Ebony or ivory,

Healthy pink or sun-kissed yellow

The colour spectrum is ignored

And we are but playgrounds

For the prancing virus

Unmasking

I breathe a sigh of relief

Each warm and stifling breath

Misting up the lens of truth

I wipe away the artificial dew

And wonder if I have to do the same

For others so they can see past the misinformation

Unmasked

The orange-tinted lies and caramel-coated numbers

Sweetened and processed for the mass to swallow

But the artificially sweeteners cannot dilute

The dark fury of those who will no longer

Remain hypnotized by the myopic normality

Masks

Blue ones, green ones, black ones, pink

The spectrum of color protection

Does not hide the worried looks

For oneself, family, and country

WHO dares to impose a biased and skewed

Politics under a shredded umbrella of protection

Straight hair, short hair, curly hair, dyed

The hairstyles at odds with the masks

Speaks of a time before a virus was king

WHO was crowned by vilifying the truthsayers

And made them repent before the king's message

Of death took them away

Worried looks, panicked actions, unjustified stigma, concerns

The raw negative emotions far outweigh care

Unconcealed and unconstrained by masks

WHO misinforms and misdirect the world

Falsely congratulating those who least deserve it

All for expediency of the lowest order

Spread of Darkness

The spread of darkness is no longer in the dead of night

It is plain to see under the glaring sun

Unafraid

Aided and abetted

Led by foppish clowns who only cares for attention

And a stuffed animal playing god

The thief of life scurries out in the open

Unimpeded by walls and roofs

Pick-pocketing our senses of well-being

Turning streets into empty roads and pavements

Where mortals fear to tread

He ignores the legal boundaries and barriers

Gleefully hopping onto ships and planes

To spread its unwanted gospel of ill will

Gaining unwilling followers to lament his coming

The thief of freedom is the freest of all

Unchallenged as he moves among us

Palming our liberty in action and engagement

Introducing howls of frustration in the virus-ruled land

Where the virus dance with abandon

He has no regard for propaganda and misinformation

(A jokester with a fatal sense of humour)

Riding these vehicles

As he tramples the power that be under his amorphous feet

Let all be wary of the thief and those

Who are selectively blind and deaf in looting spree

Ouroboros

We use attempted virus to prevent the pandemic
We seek understand naturally by generating more waste
The irony is heavy, it weighs on my soul
But the soulless clowns and iron-fisted powermongers
Quantitatively cut the guilt away
How shameless we con ourselves

The scamster scams its own
Finding satisfaction in pointless numbers
When you own more than the seconds in your life
Life becomes a game you ruin others by

The herald of nature stops
the industrial complex
In its tracks
Give passes
to the plundering and inflation of black gold

WHO misinforms and misdirect the world

Falsely congratulating those who least deserve it

All for expediency of the lowest order

Spread of Darkness

The spread of darkness is no longer in the dead of night

It is plain to see under the glaring sun

Unafraid

Aided and abetted

Led by foppish clowns who only cares for attention

And a stuffed animal playing god

The thief of life scurries out in the open

Unimpeded by walls and roofs

Pick-pocketing our senses of well-being

Turning streets into empty roads and pavements

Where mortals fear to tread

He ignores the legal boundaries and barriers

Gleefully hopping onto ships and planes

To spread its unwanted gospel of ill will

Gaining unwilling followers to lament his coming

The thief of freedom is the freest of all

Unchallenged as he moves among us

Palming our liberty in action and engagement

Introducing howls of frustration in the virus-ruled land

Where the virus dance with abandon

He has no regard for propaganda and misinformation

(A jokester with a fatal sense of humour)

Riding these vehicles

As he tramples the power that be under his amorphous feet

Let all be wary of the thief and those

Who are selectively blind and deaf in looting spree

Ouroboros

We use attenuated virus to prevent the pandemic

We seek understand nature by generating more waste

The irony is heavy, it weighs on my soul

But the soulless clowns and iron-fisted powermongers

Quantitatively ease the guilt away

How shameless we con ourselves

The scamster scams its own

Finding satisfaction in pointless numbers

When you own more than the seconds in your life

Life becomes a game you ruin others by

The herald of nature stops

the industrial complex

In its tracks

Give pauses

to the plundering and reliance of black gold

Life flows back to the City of Canals

Languidly walking on empty streets

The masters of the planet is busy devouring themselves

New Year

Getting away from the hustle and bustle of the old street

Staying away from the crowds on the light rail

The quiet Tamsui

Is more rural than the countryside

The two-lane road

Pretending to be thin all year

Only when all the cars go home for the New Year

Does it admits

"Actually, I am a four-lane street"

Stray dog lying on the asphalt

Give me a silly stare as I ride my bicycle

New year old year it doesn't matter

The sea breeze and drizzle here

Is only share by it and I

Fire crackers in full bloom

Cherry blossoms in full bloom

Traditions competing with nature

To see whose New Year's event

Is more appealing

I Know

I know

From the arc of the eyebrows

The little wrinkles around the corner

Of the smiling eyes

That it's you

I know

From the muffled voice

The fact I don't remember what the

Bottom of your face looks like

That you care

I know

The time is not what we expect

Not what we hoped for

But hope is what we expect

To get us through the times

I know

Science and sanity

Not politics and populism

Will be the weapon

To prevail against the invisible enemy

All this I know

And thus I know we shall

Survive the circle of life

Only to begin again

Overcast

Gray sky streaked with silvery rain

It is the tears of memory

From the city that remembers past visits

I tried to pick up the glistening heavenly gems

But they slipped through my fingers.

O! They don't belong to me

I let them lie

Hoping that someone else

Can pick them up

To live the joy that

I once knew

Early Autumn · Tamsui

Early autumn

Drizzle comes chasing

After the typhoon

Expelling the extreme heat

But cannot drive away

The heat under the mask

Tamkang

Students

Returns to campus

With autumn days

Virtual classrooms

Cannot replace

Physical enthusiasm

Tamsui's

Old streets

Leaning against

The river's shoulders

The vendors' whispering

Lamenting only viruses

Are reverberating in the streets

The Setting Sun in South Africa

The bloody sun falling back

Onto the parched horizon

Pumping and dripping

My agony onto the land that

Deserves greater mercy

From the inhumane humans

Take the possession and wealth

But you cannot sell his life

To any lifemonger

So for what did you strip

the soul from the body

That did you no harm

Two Places

The man-made time

Whipping, driving life

I live in parallel timelines

Waking up with Tamsui

Looking at the previous night's

Early African morning

The crescent moon

Looked confusingly

At me standing in the cold wind

The luxury of dreaming

Has burst like a bubble

Pine leaves communicate

In whispers with the night owl

The night scene hypnotizes

To be carved into the heart and eyes

The soul living in the Dark Continent

Support the body of the Far East

The brutal reality

Tears apart the sense of security

Of the two places

Autumn Tiger

This year's autumn tiger

Is short-lived

Did it seek

The Cheshire Cat's tutelage

Leaving only a mocking smile behind

Or was it hunted and put down

By the man-made climate change

Leaving nothing behind

Buddha Worship in South Africa

The deity lost in a strange land

In lotus position, wise eyes looking

Into the Highveld

He cannot find himself

For even he does not know how to pronounce

The location: Bronkhorstspruit

I bowed and kowtow because of tradition

And respect for those who brought him here

Faith is now an empty concept

But I ask not for the sake of my peace of mind

But at the behest of my parents

Who had left too soon

So that they won't be lost on a long-inhabited

Yet unfamiliar land

Black Forest Cake

My constant craving

For the black forest

Cake that haunt my dreams

Reminds me of what I'm missing

The fork slices through

Fresh cream and dark chocolate

Reflex tear and saliva

Wets my face

Are the secretions joy or sadness

For tasting the old familiar taste

I don't know nor care

Except for the fact that heaven is rolling down my tongue

Lawn I

The Taiwanese lawn is inimical

Accompanied by kagemusha weeds

To prevent the unexpected bare feet

Suddenly assassinating the emerald lord

Because their relatives who were friendly with humans

Have already been eradicated

Lawn II

The South African lawn stands parched

Mixed with the brown soil in the distant vision

My bare feet stamp on their corpses of this year

Reminiscing their rebirth in spring next year

Perhaps my optimism and hopes

Will resprout with them

Flight

The sweet potato-shaped democracy

Not yet fully fledged but trying hard to fly

Carries the hopes, dreams and expectations

Of those on it and away from it

Learn from Daedulus

Build your own wings and fly

But do not lose sight of the freedom

And confuse not the warmth of liberty

With the impassioned heat of those

Who have no wings

Small Happiness

Waking up in the wintry cold

Sweating under the unrelenting sun

I am grateful

For I am alive

On the island

Convenience stores stare out from every corner

Dozing commuters rides the out-stretching arterials

I am thankful

For I am free to move

On the island

Uncensored information flies at me

On the wings of wifi

I am happy

For I can know the real world

On the island

Free to walk and talk and think

These are not small happiness

When they nurtures the souls

On the island

Dream · Love

I am intact

I am missing

I walk on a familiar path

That ends in the unknown

You were there

With pieces I did not know

I was missing

I tried to pick it up

But they did not belong to me

The love remains in the dream

I am whole outside

I am fragmented inside

Original Name

The freshwater of Tamsui

Lightly passes

And lingers in the mangroves

By the foot of Guanyin Mountain

The fiddler crabs

Strolling on the mud

Wave their instruments and ask

Have the poet arrived

The osmanthus flowers of osmanthus alley

Once again missed the visiting poetic feelings

But the villagers' passion

Are on their faces

Blooming like flowers

The enchanting feelings of the countryside and poetry

Float on the poetry road

The water source of Shuiyuanli

Hides in the mists of Datun Mountain

I cannot find it

And can only ask the water bamboos in the paddy

Whether the crystal clear water

Tastes as sweet as nectar

Passing on Poetry

The limitless knowledge

On old and yellowed pages

On the brand new cloud

Watching new members joining them

The vibrant fonts of poetry

Brings centuries of experiences

Walks into the hall on Tiger Hill

The poetic connotations are no longer in a moment

But a part of infinity

Lighthouse

Climbing the lighthouse that no longer exists

Observing the past

The steel bone weary fort

Insists on safeguarding

The art and culture of the countryside

In the sincere singsong voice

One sees

One reveals

The longing for the future

Amidst the fog of authoritarianism

Become the lighthouse of culture

Shine and brighten the poetic feelings in the sea and the land

Waltz Politik

One two three

Left step

Right step

Back step

The splendorous steps

The government dances

Always moving

Never progressing

One two three

Promising prices will most certainly not go up

Raising the cost of the living

Excusing the time are different

Don't lose the rhythm

One two three

Abortion is not a choice

Gun equals freedom

Justice turns political

Keep the waltz going

One two three

Left right back

Round and round we go

When will this dance end?

Blue and Gold

Blue sky

Golden field

Tainted by the gray smoky

Streams of tanks

Soldiers

And missile

Of never good news

Spawning death

Of themselves and those

Thought to be their siblings and cousins

Rivulets of injustice and loss

Streaming into online torrents

Watering the bread basket of Europe

With blood and propaganda

Now a broken sieve trying to retain

The fragments of peace

The wheat waves forlorn goodbyes

To the blue whispering streams

And golden halcyon days

But it knows the independence once won

Will never again be trampled

By the hooves of horseriding dictators

Festivals —— Winter I

The northeastern wind brought the
Letters stained by the undying viruses
In the unliving smog
And the news that he know who has been
Naughty or nice
But the saint is wary of the porcupine island
And guides his reindeers around the missiles
Staring into the Nativity play
That gives birth to no peace of mind

Jingles on endless loops
The First Noel sang by unfeeling machines
The commercialized pagan festival
Continues to attract more pagans
Who burns no candles
But swipe screens to seek the holiday spirit

Christmas is not so merry when

Peace on Earth and goodwill towards all men

Are only found on the pages of

Made-up stories.

Festivals —— Winter II

The wet and the wind buffets the crowd
Relentlessly charging towards freedom
The freedom to forget the deaths
The freedom to scream without a mask
Breaking free of the shackles beset
Upon them by microbial oppressors
Celebrate with empty pieces of paper and
Sterilize memory with the firework
Spewing from the skyscrapers and bridges
Flowing against the swarming bodies
Shouting happy new year quietly to myself
Amidst the mental fireworks

Taiwan Days, South Africa Nights

I wake up and move

With packs of my own skin colour

My mind swims with and against the swarm

The Highveld thunderstorm 11000 km away

Rings louder in my ears

Than the zooming scooter that

Just missed my toes

The Formosan sun and humidity

Drain my will

I wish for an African shade

Under jacaranda trees

To cool and revitalize me

Like Merlin of Amber

Walking the Earth and the shadow

I move in two worlds

Dodging the death of my unknown self

Trying to leave behind bad blood and history

The genesis of new humour and narratives

Substitute for the worn-out thoughts and corpuscles

The new person created from within

A clone I am of the older me

Wearing the same skin

Brainwashing myself with

My old real and made up memories

I turn off my lights

Turn on the air-con

And dreams of the rolling blackouts

That haunts my old life

I live in a duality

Of wakefulness and sleep

Taiwan day South Africa night

South Africa day Taiwan night

Night day

South Taiwan Africa

The duality is united in me

About the poet / translator

Te-chang Mike Lo, born 1978 in Taiwan. He immigrated as a child to South Africa with his family where he resided for over 25 years and obtained a PhD in molecular medicine. After returning to Taiwan to find his Taiwaneseness, a series of serendipitous events turned his career path to interpreting / translating / teaching and writing. He currently resides in Tamsui in northern Taiwan, working at further sharpening his writing skills.

語言文學類　PG2994　台灣詩叢20

台灣日‧南非夜
Taiwan Days, South Africa Nights
——羅得彰漢英雙語詩集

著　　譯 / 羅得彰（Te-chang Mike Lo）
叢書策劃 / 李魁賢（Lee Kuei-shien）
責任編輯 / 陳彥儒
圖文排版 / 黃莉珊
封面設計 / 王嵩賀

發 行 人 / 宋政坤
法律顧問 / 毛國樑　律師
出版發行 / 秀威資訊科技股份有限公司
　　　　　114台北市內湖區瑞光路76巷65號1樓
　　　　　電話：+886-2-2796-3638　傳真：+886-2-2796-1377
　　　　　http://www.showwe.com.tw
劃撥帳號 / 19563868　戶名：秀威資訊科技股份有限公司
　　　　　讀者服務信箱：service@showwe.com.tw
展售門市 / 國家書店（松江門市）
　　　　　104台北市中山區松江路209號1樓
　　　　　電話：+886-2-2518-0207　傳真：+886-2-2518-0778
網路訂購 / 秀威網路書店：https://store.showwe.tw
　　　　　國家網路書店：https://www.govbooks.com.tw

2023年9月　BOD一版
定價：200元
版權所有　翻印必究
本書如有缺頁、破損或裝訂錯誤，請寄回更換

讀者回函卡

國家圖書館出版品預行編目

台灣日.南非夜：羅得彰漢英雙語詩集 = Taiwan
days, South Africa nights/羅得彰著譯. --
一版. -- 臺北市：秀威資訊科技股份有限公司,
2023.09
    面；　公分. -- (語言文學類；PG2994)(台灣
詩叢；20)
　BOD版
　ISBN 978-626-7346-22-8(平裝)

863.51   112012713